D1626230

MEET ALL THESE FRIENDS IN BUZZ BOOKS:

Thomas the Tank Engine
Fireman Sam
The Animals of Farthing Wood
Skeleton Warriors
Puppy In My Pocket
Kitty In My Pocket
Pony In My Pocket

First published in Great Britain in 1996 by Buzz Books
an imprint of Reed Children's Books
Michelin House, 81 Fulham Road, London SW3 6RB
and Auckland, Melbourne, Singapore and Toronto.

Based on a Martin Gates Production
Copyright ©1996 BMG Entertainment
Licensed by Just Licensing Ltd
Text copyright © 1996 Reed International Books Limited
Illustrations by Arkadia copyright © 1996 Reed International Books Limited

ISBN 1 85591 554 5

Printed in Italy

Toad in Trouble

Story by Katie Vandyck

from the animated series

One summer's day, as Rat and Mole were having breakfast, a stern-faced Badger walked through the door.

"The time has come," he said, firmly.

He reminded the animals of their intention to cure Toad of his passion for motor-cars. Toad's craze had brought him nothing but trouble but it seemed he could not give them up.

The three animals set off for Toad Hall and arrived just as Toad was stepping into yet another brand new motor-car.

"Take him inside," called Badger.

Rat and Mole dragged the protesting Toad into Toad Hall and locked him in his room. He would be kept under constant guard until he was cured.

Toad, however, was determined to escape. Whilst Badger and Mole were out on business one day, Toad managed to persuade the kindly Rat that he was very ill indeed. With pale cheeks and quivering voice, he begged Rat to fetch his lawyer and his doctor. When Rat had gone Toad tied his sheets together into a rope and escaped out of the bedroom window.

"Smart piece of work that!" he laughed as he sauntered into town.

He was just ordering a large lunch at the local inn when he heard the unmistakable "Poop poop!" of a motor-car. A wild look came into his eyes, and he crept outside and saw an empty vehicle standing in the yard.

"Can't be any harm in my just looking at it!" he said as he cranked the engine, engaged the gears and zoomed out onto the road.

Some time later as Toad stood in the courtroom, head bowed with shame, he knew that this time he had gone too far. The Chief Magistrate addressed the courtroom.

"The incorrigible rogue we see before us has been found guilty of stealing a motor-car, driving to the public danger and, most seriously, of gross impertinence to the rural police."

"Ooooh," murmured the courtroom, shocked at Toad's behaviour.

The clerk of the court suggested that twenty years in prison might be a suitable punishment. There was an enthusiastic round of applause.

"An excellent suggestion!" cried the Magistrate. A shocked Toad was dragged from the courtroom and taken to a castle where he was locked away.

"Oh, stupid animal that I have been; this is the end of everything," moaned Toad in his dark prison cell. The Gaoler's daughter took pity on the miserable creature. She brought him food and listened patiently to endless tales about himself. One day she came in looking thoughtful.

"Listen, Toad, my Aunt is a washerwoman. She could let you have her dress and bonnet and you could escape in disguise."

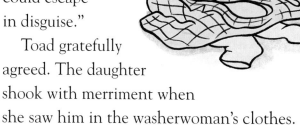

Toad gratefully agreed. The daughter shook with merriment when she saw him in the washerwoman's clothes.

"You're the very image of her," she laughed. "Now goodbye, Toad, and good luck."

Toad dodged passed the prison warden, and scuttled across the castle yard to freedom.

Late that afternoon Toad came upon a railway station. He examined the train timetable eagerly.

"What luck. A train in ten minutes!" he cried.

Then he realised with horror that he had left his wallet behind in the prison. He began to sob.

The train driver, thinking that Toad was an old washerwoman, took pity on him.

"If you'll wash a few shirts for me, I'll give you a ride on my engine," he suggested kindly.

Toad leapt onto the train. He was saved! He hummed merrily to himself as the train gathered speed and dusk fell around them.

A little while later, the driver looked back over his shoulder and seemed puzzled.

"There's an engine on our rails, coming along at a great pace. It looks as if we are being pursued," he said, frowning.

"Oh, oh, no – no," moaned Toad.

Sure enough, close behind them was a
train crowded with warders and policemen
all shaking sticks and shouting, "Stop, stop!"

Toad begged the train driver to save him.
As they exited a tunnel, the driver ordered
Toad to jump. As he rolled down the bank
to freedom, Toad could see the other train
gaining fast.

The next morning Toad was walking
alongside a canal when he heard a friendly
greeting from a passing barge.

"A nice morning, ma'am," called the
barge woman.

Realising that she believed him to be a
washerwoman, Toad spun her a woeful tale
and was offered a lift. Toad boasted that his
was the finest laundry business in the whole

country. He claimed
that he was never so
happy as when he had
two arms in a tub.

"Then perhaps you'll allow me to give
you a little treat. It'll be a big help to me
and I'll know you're enjoying yourself,"
smiled the barge woman, pointing to a huge
pile of dirty laundry.

Toad stared in horror at the washing, but knew he had no choice but to get it done. The barge woman rolled around with laughter as she watched Toad, covered with soap suds and soaked to the skin, struggle with the tangle of clothes. This made Toad very angry. He shouted that she was a common, low, fat barge woman and he was a well-known Toad.

"Why, so you are," she replied, picking him up by the leg and hurling him into the water.

Toad hauled himself out of the canal and onto the towpath. He hastily untied the barge horse, leapt on its back and galloped away down a lane.

"Toad triumphs again!" he cried.

Toad was becoming rather hungry when he chanced upon a gypsy, sitting by his caravan, contemplating a steaming pot of savoury stew. Toad felt his mouth watering. The gypsy eyed him carefully.

"Want to sell that horse of yours?" he asked.

Toad had an idea. He would sell the horse for a little money and a great deal of stew. At first he pretended not to be interested.

"What? Me sell this beautiful young horse of mine? I'm far too fond of him, and he simply dotes on me."

The gypsy looked at him incredulously and made him an offer. Toad declined; but before long they had agreed on a price and Toad left on foot, filled to the brim with stew.

As he
neared home,
Toad heard the
most beautiful
sound in the
world: the
"Poop poop!"
of a motor-car.

As it drew up beside him he realised in
panic that it was the very one he had stolen,
with the same occupants. Far from
recognising Toad, however, the three in the
car believed him to be a poor old
washerwoman and offered him a lift. He
persuaded them to let him drive.

"Fancy a washerwoman driving so well,"
they remarked to each other.

All at once Toad lost his head and
slammed his foot down on the accelerator.

As the car sped off the wind whipped Toad's bonnet back to reveal his true identity. Toad was discovered!

As soon as they realised who he was the passengers tried to grab him. The car swerved off the road and Toad went sailing into the air.

He landed with a bump, clambered to his feet and escaped across the fields, laughing at his success. Suddenly he realised he was being followed. He turned to see the chauffeur and two large policemen racing towards him.

"Oh, what an ass I am! What a conceited and heedless ass!" he cried.

The policemen were gaining on him; he lost his footing, fell through a hedge and landed with a loud splash in the river.

Hurtling helplessly downstream, he tried desperately to grasp the reeds and rushes that grew along the water's edge, but the stream was so strong that it tore them out of his hands. At last he managed to grab hold of a tree root and came to a stop in front of a hole in the river bank.

Toad hauled himself up out of the water and was able to rest his elbows on the edge of the hole. There he remained, puffing and panting, for he was quite exhausted. At last he sighed and looked about him. As he peered into the hole he could see two bright eyes gleaming up at him. It was Rat. He was safe at last.